CROWD

HOIST

SWING

MIKE MULLIGAN

AND HIS STEAM SHOVEL

MIKE MULLIGAN
AND HIS
STEAM SHOVEL

STORY AND PICTURES BY VIRGINIA LEE BURTON

HOUGHTON MIFFLIN COMPANY · BOSTON

www.houghtonmifflinbooks.com

LIBRÁRY OF CONGRESS CATALOG CARD NUMBER 39-30335
ISBN: 0-395-16961-5 REINFORCED EDITION
ISBN: 0-395-25939-8 SANDPIPER EDITON

Printed in China

SCP   100 99 98
4500368296

TO

MIKE

Mike Mulligan had a steam shovel,
  a beautiful red steam shovel.
    Her name was Mary Anne.
      Mike Mulligan was very proud of Mary Anne.
        He always said that she could dig as much in a day
          as a hundred men could dig in a week,
            but he had never been quite sure
              that this was true.

3

Mike Mulligan and Mary Anne
had been digging together
for years and years.
Mike Mulligan took such good care
of Mary Anne
she never grew old.

It was Mike Mulligan and Mary Anne
    and some others
  who dug the great canals
    for the big boats
      to sail through.

It was Mike Mulligan
and Mary Anne
and some others
who cut through
the high mountains
so that trains
could go through.

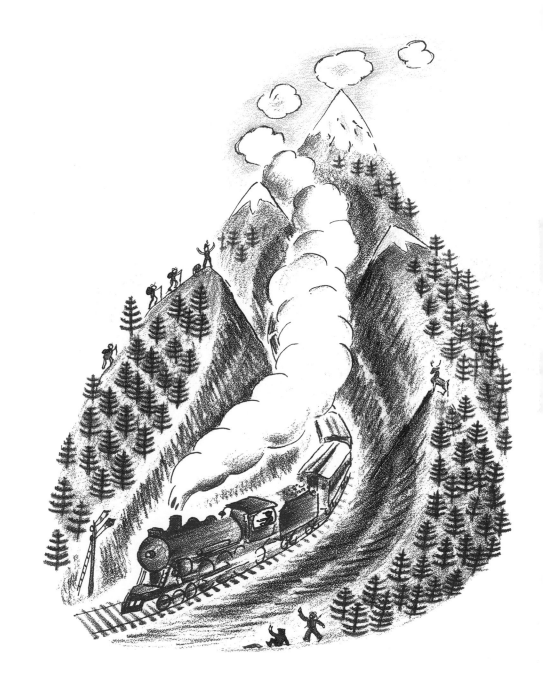

It was Mike Mulligan and Mary Anne
and some others
who lowered the hills
and straightened the curves

8

to make the long highways
for the automobiles.

It was Mike Mulligan
and Mary Anne
and some others
who smoothed out the ground
and filled in the holes

to make the landing fields
for the airplanes.

And it was Mike Mulligan
and Mary Anne
and some others
who dug the deep holes
for the cellars
of the tall skyscrapers
in the big cities.
When people used to stop
and watch them,
Mike Mulligan and Mary Anne
used to dig a little faster
and a little better.
The more people stopped,
the faster and better they dug.
Some days they would keep
as many as thirty-seven trucks
busy taking away the dirt they had dug.

Then along came
   the new gasoline shovels
     and the new electric shovels
      and the new Diesel motor shovels
       and took all the jobs away from the steam shovels.

14

Mike Mulligan

and Mary Anne

were

VERY

SAD.

All the other steam shovels were being sold for junk,
or left out in old gravel pits to rust and fall apart.

16   Mike loved Mary Anne.   He couldn't do that to her.

He had taken
such good care of her
that she could still dig
as much in a day
as a hundred men
could dig in a week;
at least he thought she could
but he wasn't quite sure.
Everywhere they went
the new gas shovels
and the new electric shovels
and the new Diesel motor shovels
had all the jobs.   No one wanted
Mike Mulligan and Mary Anne any more.
Then one day Mike read in a newspaper that the town
of Popperville was going to build a new town hall.
'We are going to dig the cellar of that town hall,'
said Mike to Mary Anne, and off they started.

They left the canals
and the railroads
and the highways
and the airports
and the big cities
where no one wanted them any more
and went away out in the country.

They crawled along slowly
up the hills and down the hills
till they came to the little town
of Popperville.

When they got there they found that the selectmen
were just deciding who should dig the cellar for the new town hall.
Mike Mulligan spoke to Henry B. Swap, one of the selectmen.
'I heard,' he said, 'that you are going
to build a new town hall.   Mary Anne and I
will dig the cellar for you in just one day.'
'What!' said Henry B. Swap.   'Dig a cellar in a day!
It would take a hundred men at least a week
to dig the cellar for our new town hall.'
'Sure,' said Mike, 'but Mary Anne can dig as much in a day
as a hundred men can dig in a week.'
Though he had never been quite sure that this was true.
Then he added,
'If we can't do it, you won't have to pay.'
Henry B. Swap thought that this would be
an easy way to get part of the cellar dug for nothing,
so he smiled in rather a mean way
and gave the job of digging the cellar of the new town hall
to Mike Mulligan and Mary Anne.

They started in
early the next morning
just as the sun was coming up.
Soon a little boy came along.
'Do you think you will finish by sundown?'
he said to Mike Mulligan.
'Sure,' said Mike, 'if you stay and watch us.
We always work faster and better
when someone is watching us.'
So the little boy stayed to watch.

Then Mrs. McGillicuddy,
Henry B. Swap,
and the Town Constable
came over to see
what was happening,
and they stayed to watch.

Mike Mulligan
and Mary Anne
dug a little faster
and a little better.

This gave the little boy a good idea.
He ran off and told the postman with the morning mail,
the telegraph boy on his bicycle,
the milkman with his cart and horse,
the doctor on his way home,
and the farmer and his family
coming into town for the day,
and they all stopped and stayed to watch.
That made Mike Mulligan and Mary Anne
dig a little faster and a little better.
They finished the first corner
neat and square . . .
but the sun was getting higher.

26

Clang! Clang! Clang!

The Fire Department arrived.

They had seen the smoke

and thought there was a fire.

Then the little boy said,

'Why don't you stay and watch?'

So the Fire Department of Popperville

stayed to watch Mike Mulligan and Mary Anne.

When they heard the fire engine, the children

in the school across the street couldn't keep

their eyes on their lessons.   The teacher called

a long recess and the whole school came out to watch.

That made Mike Mulligan and Mary Anne

dig still faster and still better.

They finished the second corner neat and square,
but the sun was right up in the top of the sky.

29

Now the girl who answers
the telephone called up the next towns
of Bangerville and Bopperville and
Kipperville and Kopperville and told them
what was happening in Popperville.
All the people came over to see
if Mike Mulligan and his steam shovel
could dig the cellar in just one day.
The more people came, the faster
Mike Mulligan and Mary Anne dug.
But they would have to hurry.
They were only halfway through
and the sun was beginning to go down.

They finished the third corner . . . neat and square.

Never had Mike Mulligan and Mary Anne
had so many people to watch them;
never had they dug so fast and so well;
and never had the sun seemed
to go down so fast.
'Hurry, Mike Mulligan!
Hurry! Hurry!'
shouted the little boy.
'There's not much more time!'
Dirt was flying everywhere,
and the smoke and steam were so thick
that the people could hardly see anything.
But listen!

BING! BANG! CRASH! SLAM!
LOUDER AND LOUDER,
FASTER AND
FASTER.

Then suddenly it was quiet.
Slowly the dirt settled down.
The smoke and steam cleared away,
and there was the cellar
all finished.

Four corners . . . neat and square;
four walls . . . straight down,
and Mike Mulligan and Mary Anne at the bottom,
and the sun was just going down behind the hill.
'Hurray!' shouted the people.   'Hurray for Mike Mulligan
and his steam shovel!   They have dug the cellar in just one day.'

Suddenly the little boy said,
  'How are they going to get out?'
  'That's right,' said Mrs. McGillicuddy
    to Henry B. Swap. 'How is he going
    to get his steam shovel out?'
    Henry B. Swap didn't answer,
      but he smiled in rather a mean way.
    Then everybody said,
      'How are they going to get out?
    'Hi! Mike Mulligan!
      How are you going to get
        your steam shovel out?'

Mike Mulligan
looked around
at the four square walls
and four square corners,
and he said,
    'We've dug so fast
        and we've dug so well
            that we've quite forgotten
                to leave a way out!'
        Nothing like this had ever happened
            to Mike Mulligan and Mary Anne before,
                and they didn't know what to do.

Nothing like this
 had ever happened before
 in Popperville.
 Everybody started
talking at once,
 and everybody had
 a different idea,
 and everybody thought
that his idea was the best.
They talked and they talked
 and they argued and they fought
 till they were worn out,
 and still no one knew how to get
 Mike Mulligan and Mary Anne
 out of the cellar they had dug.
 Then Henry B. Swap said,
 'The job isn't finished because
Mary Anne isn't out of the cellar,
so Mike Mulligan won't get paid.'
And he smiled again in a rather mean way.

Now the little boy,
who had been keeping very quiet,
had another good idea.
He said,
'Why couldn't we leave Mary Anne in the cellar
and build the new town hall above her?
Let her be the furnace for the new town hall *
and let Mike Mulligan be the janitor.
Then you wouldn't have to buy a new furnace,
and we could pay Mike Mulligan
for digging the cellar
in just one day.'

39

* Acknowledgments to Dickie Birkenbush.

'Why not?' said Henry B. Swap,
and smiled in a way
that was not quite so mean.
'Why not?' said Mrs. McGillicuddy.
'Why not?' said the Town Constable.
'Why not?' said all the people.
So they found a ladder
and climbed down into the cellar
to ask Mike Mulligan and Mary Anne.

40

'Why not?' said Mike Mulligan.
So it was decided,
and everybody was happy.

They built the new town hall
right over Mike Mulligan and Mary Anne.
It was finished before winter.

Every day the little boy goes over to see
Mike Mulligan and Mary Anne,
and Mrs. McGillicuddy takes him
nice hot apple pies.   As for Henry B. Swap,
he spends most of his time in the cellar
of the new town hall listening to the stories
that Mike Mulligan has to tell
and smiling in a way that isn't mean at all.

Now when you go to Popperville,
be sure to go down in the cellar
of the new town hall.
There they'll be,
Mike Mulligan and Mary Anne . . .
Mike in his rocking chair
smoking his pipe,
and Mary Anne beside him,
warming up the meetings
in the new town hall.

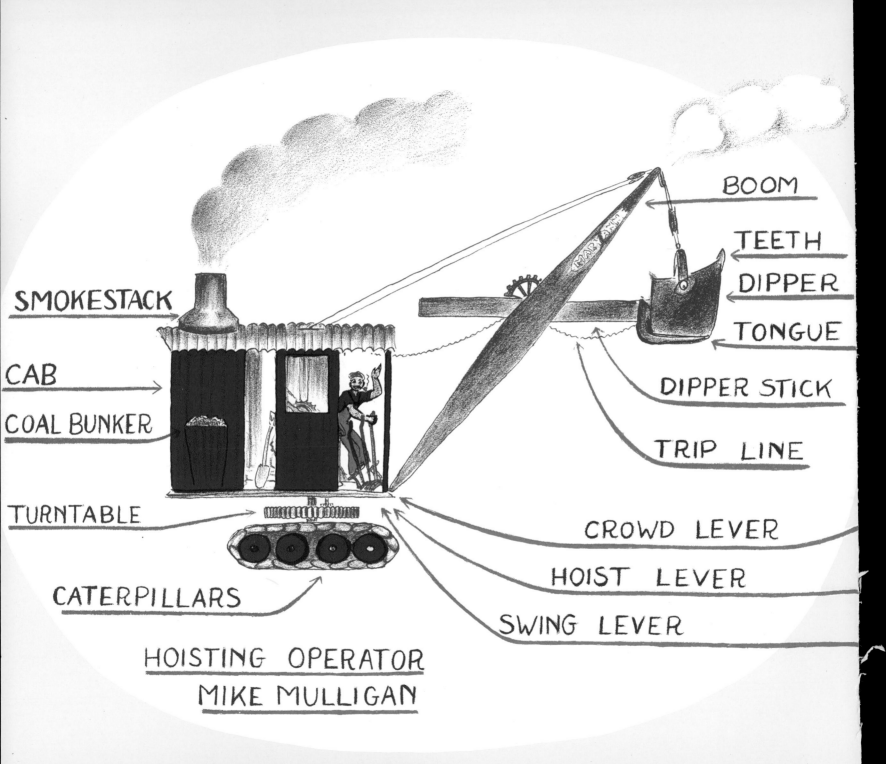